CARING FOR YOUR LION

Congratulations on your new lion! We know you ordered a kitten, but we ran out of those.

Luckily, a lion is practically the same thing!

Caring for your lion is easy. Just follow this handy guide.

Caring for Your Lion

by Tammi Sauer
illustrated by Troy Cummings

SCHOLASTIC INC.

Pop!

STEP 2

Locate the enclosed feather. Keep it handy in case of an emergency.

STEP 3

Try very hard NOT to look like a zebra. Or a gazelle. Or a bunny.

(See Diagram A.)

A.

STEP 4

If you ignored STEP 3, you are probably sitting inside a lion right now. No problem! Simply use your feather.

(See Diagrams B, C, D, and E.)

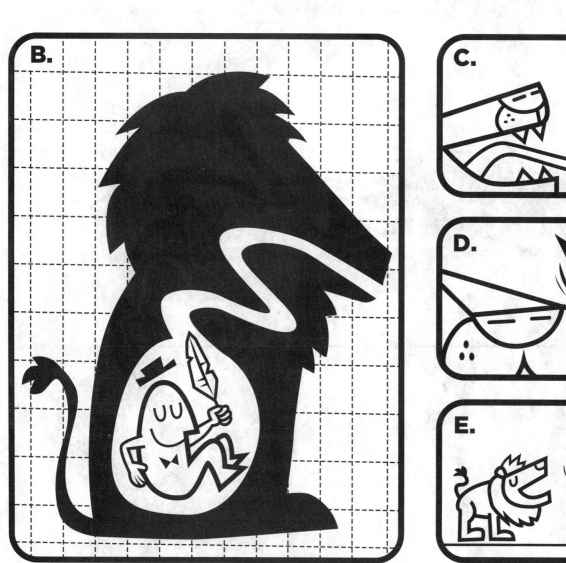

B.

C.

D.

E.

STEP 5

Order ten large pizzas and promptly feed your lion.

When your lion accidentally swallows the pizza delivery guy, you know what to do!

STEP 6

Potty train your lion.
It's a cinch with the
Deluxe Lion Potty Pack.

(Some assembly required. See Diagram F.)

F.

TOOLS NEEDED:

SCOOP-DE-DOO
CAT LITTER
100 lbs

STEP 7

Provide your lion with space to play.

Your lion loves to nap. Be ready for him to doze off just about anywhere.

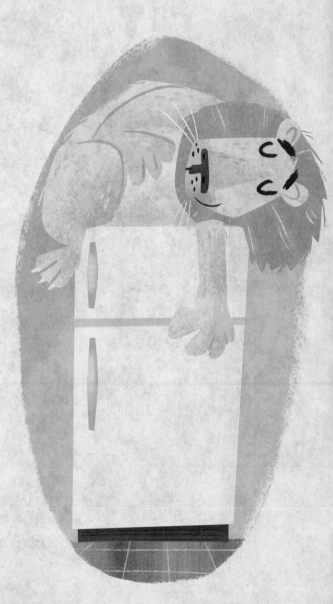

ROOOO

STEP 9

Give your lion an occasional treat—especially when he does something good.

At bath time, fill the tub with equal parts water and lion. Then add a smidge of bubble bath. Be sure to have your camera ready for some adorable photos!

drip

GOOSH!

Post-bath, your lion is half his normal size.
Do. Not. Panic.
Simply grab a blow dryer and get busy.
(Expect a teensy bit of shedding.)

STEP **12**

At the end of a full day,
your lion is sleepy.
Prepare a cozy bed for him.

Realize your lion is the purrrrr-fect pet for you.

For Mason. —T. S.

**For Edie: the fiercest, furriest, fang-iest
member of the family. —T. C.**

ISBN 978-1-338-56854-7

12 11 10 9 8 7 6 5 4 3 2 1   19 20 21 22 23 24

Printed in the U.S.A.   40

First Scholastic printing, April 2019

The artwork for this book was created digitally.
Art direction and design by Jo Obarowski

Tammi Sauer is the author of many picture books, including *Chicken Dance, Cowboy Camp, Mary Had a Little Glam, Your Alien Returns,* and *Your Alien*, which earned starred reviews in both *Kirkus* and *Publishers Weekly*. She is a former teacher and library media specialist who now celebrates reading and writing with thousands of kids each year through her author visits. Tammi and her family live in Edmond, Oklahoma. They have one dog, two geckos, and a tank full of random fish, but so far, no lions.

Troy Cummings grew up surrounded by animals: cats, dogs, chickens, ducks, a hermit crab, a parakeet, and a couple of wild siblings. He now writes and illustrates children's books, including The Notebook of Doom series, *Giddy-Up, Daddy!,* and *The Twelve Days of Christmas in Indiana*. Troy lives in Indiana with his wife and kiddos.

(And no lions. Yet.)